Goodnight STORIES

Contents

- Goldilocks and the Three Bears
- Little Red Riding Hood
- Thumbelina
- Cinderella
- Snow White
- Beauty and the Beast
- The Emperor's New Clothes
- The Princess and the Pea

Goldilocks and the Three Bears

One Sunday morning the three bears were in their garden. Suddenly, Baby Bear cried out, "Hurray! I've caught a fish. Please, Mama, will you fry the fish?"

"Yes, I will, but now it's time for breakfast," said Mama Bear.

Mama Bear went into the kitchen to make breakfast. She put a pot on the fire and began to make porridge.

Just then Baby Bear came in. He took out his bowl from the cupboard and said, "Mama, I'm hungry. May I have some porridge? I love porridge."

"Yes, of course you may," said Mama Bear. "But it is very hot."

"Let us take a walk in the woods while the porridge cools down," said Papa Bear. So the bears went out for a walk. On the way Baby Bear met his friends the rabbit, the birds and the butterflies.

Soon after the bears had left, a little girl came to their house. She had lovely golden hair and was called Goldilocks. She had gone out for a walk and had lost her way in the woods.

She went up to the house and knocked on the door, but no one opened it.

Goldilocks opened the door and peeped inside. She looked around the room but could not see anyone.

On the wall was a picture of three bears. And on the table were three bowls of delicious-smelling porridge. She began to feel very hungry.

Goldilocks put a spoonful of porridge from the biggest bowl in her mouth. "Oh, this is too hot," said Goldilocks. Then she tasted a little from the medium-sized bowl. It was too cold. The porridge from the smallest bowl was just right and Goldilocks ate it all up.

In the living room she saw three chairs. She sat on the biggest chair. It was too hard. Then she sat on the medium-sized chair. It was too soft.

"I think this small chair will be just right for me," she said. But when she sat on it, the chair broke and she fell down.

Now Goldilocks was feeling very sleepy. She went into the bedroom and saw three beds. She lay down on the smallest bed, covered herself with a quilt and fell asleep.

Meanwhile, the three bears were returning from their walk in the woods.

When the three bears went back home they found the gate wide open.

"Oh, we forgot to close the gate," said Papa Bear.

"Even the door is open," said Baby Bear, pointing at the door. Everybody was surprised.

The three bears rushed into the house. They saw porridge spilt on the table.

"Somebody has been eating my porridge," said Papa Bear.

"Somebody has been eating my porridge too," said Mama Bear.

"My bowl is empty!" cried Baby Bear.

The three bears then went into the living room. "Somebody has been sitting on my chair," said Papa Bear.

"Somebody has been sitting on my chair," said Mama Bear.

"My chair is broken," said Baby Bear and he began to cry.

"Let us go and check in the bedroom," said Papa Bear.

There they saw a little girl sleeping on Baby Bear's bed. Baby Bear woke her up. Goldilocks was frightened to see the bears looking at her. She got up from the bed and ran away into the woods.

Little Red Riding Hood

There once lived a little girl in a little village. Everyone loved her, for she was cheerful and good and always helped her mother around the house.

But it was her grandmother who loved her the most. Granny lived in a village on the other side of the woods.

On her birthday, Granny gave the little girl a lovely gift. It was a red riding cape with a hood.

"Thank you, Granny!" said the little girl. She loved the cape and wore it all the time. So her mother began calling her Little Red Riding Hood.

One day her mother packed a basket of sandwiches, biscuits and fruits.

"Granny is ill. Take this to her," she said, handing the basket to Little Red Riding Hood. "And be careful when you go through the woods. Keep to the path and do not talk to any strangers."

Little Red Riding Hood sang and danced as she went through the woods. A wolf asked her where she was going.

"I am taking some food for Granny," she replied. "She lives in the next village."

"Pick some flowers for her too," said the wolf.

Little Red Riding Hood began picking flowers. The wolf then rushed to Granny's cottage.

He peeped through the window and saw Granny in bed. She was reading a book. He knocked on the door.

"Come in, the door is open," said Granny.

The wolf came in quietly and pounced on Granny. She cried out and tried to run away.

But the wolf pushed her into the cupboard and locked it. Then he put on her blue nightcap and got into bed.

He pulled the quilt over himself and waited for Little Red Riding Hood.

When Little Red Riding Hood entered the cottage, she saw Granny and said, "What big eyes you have, Granny!"

"The better to see you with, my dear," said the wolf.

"And what big ears you have!" she said.

"The better to hear you with," said the cunning old wolf.

"What big teeth you have, Granny," said Little Red Riding Hood.

The wolf licked his lips and said, "The better to eat you with!" and jumped out of bed.

Little Red Riding Hood cried out, dropped the basket and ran.

The wolf caught the little girl, gobbled her up in one gulp, got back into bed and went to sleep.

A hunter passing by heard the little girl cry out. He saw the cottage door open. He went in and saw a dropped basket of food and the wolf fast asleep.

The hunter knew at once that the wolf must have gobbled up the little girl. He stamped loudly on the floor.

The wolf woke up and saw the hunter with his gun. His mouth fell open in surprise and Little Red Riding Hood popped out.

The hunter shot the wolf and he fell down dead. Then Little Red Riding Hood and the hunter searched everywhere for Granny.

They found her inside the cupboard. Little Red Riding Hood smiled and said, "Oh, Granny, I'm so glad you're safe!"

Just then, Little Red Riding Hood's mother came in looking for her.

Little Red Riding Hood told her the whole story. Then she got the plates of sandwiches and biscuits, the teapot and the cups.

They all sat down at the table for tea.

Thumbelina

Once upon a time, there lived a woman who was very lonely and longed to have a child of her own. She spent all her time in her lovely garden, sowing and watering the plants.

"How I wish I had a child to love and care for," she sighed.

One day, while she was working in the garden, an old woman visited her. "Why do you look sad, my dear?" she said.

"I have no children. I am so lonely," said the woman.

"Sow this magic seed in a pot tonight," said the old woman. "In the morning, you will have the child you want so much."

The woman sowed the seed in a pot, watered it and left it by the window.

When she woke up the next day, she was delighted to find that the seed had grown into a plant with a small yellow bud. As she looked, the bud bloomed into a lovely flower. And kneeling on the flower was a tiny girl!

"Oh!" cried the woman. "You are as small as my thumb! So I shall call you Thumbelina."

She made Thumbelina a bed out of a walnut shell and lined it with soft cotton. Every night, she kissed Thumbelina and tucked her into her bed by the window.

One night there was a terrible storm. A strong gust of wind shook the branches of the trees. The wind blew Thumbelina's shell out of the open window into the lily pond just below. Thumbelina fell out of her bed on to a leaf. She lay there, fast asleep.

A family of toads lived beside the lily pond. Next morning, when the sun came up, Mother Toad hopped around the pond, looking for flies. Suddenly she saw Thumbelina curled up fast asleep on a lily leaf.

"What a pretty little bride she will make for my son!" she croaked.

Mother Toad hopped away to call her son. Thumbelina woke up and was amazed to find two toads staring at her. She screamed in fear as they began pushing the lily leaf towards the tall weeds at the edge of the pond.

"Don't be afraid," croaked Mother Toad. But Thumbelina went on screaming.

A butterfly heard Thumbelina's cries. He swooped down and said to her, "Quick! Climb up on my back!"

The butterfly took her to the house of a kind old mouse who lived at the foot of a large tree. When Thumbelina told him that she had no home, he invited her to live with him.

One day, an old mole visited the mouse. He had a long snout and smoked a pipe. He liked Thumbelina and wanted to marry her.

The mole took her to see the tunnel under the ground where he lived. Thumbelina did not like the mole's house. It was cold and dark.

In the mole's house, Thumbelina saw a swallow who was hurt. An eagle flying past had dropped him on a thorny bush and the mole had brought him home.

Thumbelina took out the thorns from the swallow's body, put some ointment on all his wounds and tied bandages around them.

Thumbelina took care of the swallow all through winter. Soon he was well again. They became good friends.

"I don't want to marry the mole," sobbed Thumbelina one day.

"Then come away with me," said the swallow, and together they flew to the land of summer.

In the land of summer, Thumbelina met a prince who was just as tiny as she was. He fell in love with her.

"Will you marry me?" he asked.

"Oh yes," replied Thumbelina.

The prince took her to meet his parents and they got married and lived happily.

Cinderella

Ella was a kind and beautiful girl.

When she was still a little girl, her mother died and her father married again. But Ella's stepmother and her two stepsisters did not like her. They made her clean the floor, cook the meals, wash the clothes and sweep the garden.

The stepsisters were unkind. Once when Ella was cleaning the fireplace, the sisters began laughing at her.

"Just look at her! She's covered with cinders! Let's call her Cinderella!" said one of the sisters.

And so Ella became Cinderella.

One day, when they were having dinner, there was a knock on the door.

"Open the door, Cinderella," said her stepmother.

The king's messenger was handing out invitations for a ball at the palace. The prince was looking for a wife.

Cinderella wanted to go to the ball. But her stepmother said, "If you go, who will do all the work? Now go to your room and sew buttons on my new gown."

Cinderella went to her room, took out a needle and some thread and sat on a chair and began sewing the buttons.

When Cinderella's stepmother and stepsisters had left for the ball, Cinderella went out into the garden. She sat under a tree and cried.

All of a sudden her fairy godmother stood before her. She had beautiful wings and was holding a magic wand.

"Don't cry, Cinderella, you too shall go to the ball," said the fairy godmother. "Now bring me a big pumpkin, six white mice and a fat rat."

Cinderella obeyed at once. She found a big pumpkin hidden among the leaves of a creeper and a fat rat behind the pillar.

The fairy tapped the pumpkin with her wand and it turned into a beautiful coach with green curtains at the windows.

The six mice turned into fine white horses and the rat became a coachman with a tall hat.

Cinderella's face lit up in wonder.

Then the fairy godmother touched Cinderella with her wand. At once her rags turned into a beautiful gown, and on her feet were lovely glass slippers.

She also had gloves on her hands, a white pearl necklace around her neck and matching earrings on her ears.

"Hurry now," said the fairy godmother. "But remember to leave the ball before the clock strikes twelve."

Cinderella was the most beautiful young lady at the ball. The prince danced with her all night. The king and queen were very happy to see such a lovely pair.

Just when the clock was about to strike twelve, Cinderella remembered her fairy godmother's words.

She ran, afraid that the prince would find out who she really was. While hurrying away, one of her glass slippers fell off.

The prince found the slipper. He looked in every town and village for the lady to whom the slipper belonged. But the slipper did not fit anyone.

Finally the prince came to Cinderella's house. Both the stepsisters tried on the slipper but it did not fit them.

Then Cinderella sat on the stool and tried the slipper. It fitted her perfectly! Her stepsisters were surprised. But the prince was very happy and asked Cinderella to marry him. She agreed and so they got married and lived happily ever after.

Snow White

One winter day, a queen sat sewing at her window. All of a sudden she pricked her finger and a drop of blood fell on the snow on the windowsill.

"I wish I had a daughter with skin as white as snow and lips as red as blood," she said to herself.

Soon the queen gave birth to a lovely baby girl with skin as white as snow and cheeks and lips as red as blood. The queen named her Snow White.

A few years later the queen died and Snow White's father got a new wife.

The new queen was jealous of Snow White because she was so beautiful.

Every day the new queen would look into her magic mirror and ask:

"Mirror, mirror, on the wall, Who's the fairest of them all?"

The mirror would reply: "You are the fairest."

But one day the mirror said: "Snow White is fairer than you."

The queen was very angry. She called her huntsman and said, "Take Snow White into the forest and kill her. I do not want to set eyes on her again. And bring back her heart in a box to show me that she is dead."

The huntsman felt sad for Snow White. But he had to obey the queen.

The next day, the huntsman took Snow White to the forest. "The queen wants to kill you," he said. "Run away and don't come back."

Then he killed a deer and took its heart to the queen.

Snow White was afraid. She ran and ran till she came to a little cottage.

In the cottage Snow White saw a table with seven tiny chairs. And on the table were seven tiny bowls with a spoon in each of them.

Along the wall, all in a row, were seven little beds.

Snow White was so tired that she lay down and went to sleep on the beds.

That evening the seven dwarfs who lived in the cottage returned home. They had gone to the mountains to dig for gold. As soon as they lit a candle, they saw a girl sleeping on the bed. They woke her up gently.

"Who are you?" they asked.

Snow White told them her sad story.

The dwarfs felt sorry for her and said, "Stay with us. You will be safe here."

Snow White was very happy. Every day, after the dwarfs left, she cooked the food and cleaned the house.

The dwarfs told her not to open the door to anyone when they were not there.

Back in the castle, the wicked queen came to know that Snow White was alive.

She dressed up as poor woman and took some poisoned apples in a bag to the little cottage. She knocked on the door.

When Snow White came out, the wicked queen tricked her into having an apple.

As soon as she took one bite from the apple, Snow White fell down dead. The dwarfs returned and found her lying on the floor.

They were very sad and began to cry. Then they put her in a glass coffin and placed it in the garden.

One day a prince came riding by on a horse. He saw Snow White lying in the coffin and fell in love with her.

As soon as he kissed her, Snow White woke up. The dwarfs were delighted.

"Will you marry me?" asked the prince.

"Oh yes!" said Snow White.

The wicked queen was very angry when she saw the picture of Snow White and the prince together in her magic mirror. She threw her wand at the mirror. The glass broke into pieces.

The prince took Snow White to his palace and they lived happily ever after.

Beauty and the Beast

Once, there was a rich merchant who had three daughters. One day, as he was leaving for a voyage, his eldest daughter asked for a casket for her jewellery. His second daughter wanted a necklace.

But Beauty, his youngest daughter, said, "I just want a red rose."

The merchant set off on his voyage. He bought a casket and a golden crown. But he could not find a red rose for Beauty anywhere. So he was very unhappy.

While he was returning home, his ship was attacked by pirates. He escaped by jumping into the sea and swimming to an island.

As soon as he was near the shore, the merchant waded out of the water and flopped down on his knees. He was tired, wet and hungry.

After resting for a while, he walked and walked till he came to a jungle. There, among the trees, he saw a magnificent castle with tall towers.

The merchant went up to the castle and knocked on the huge arched door. When there was no reply, he pushed it open and walked in.

He saw a courtyard with rows of bushes, green lawns and crystal fountains.

"Is there anybody home?" the merchant called out. There was no answer.

He climbed up a grand staircase and found himself in a large hall.

Suddenly, a table laden with food appeared before him. There were delicious chops with gravy, mashed potatoes, salad and pudding.

The merchant was very hungry. He sat down and ate his fill.

Just then, he saw some red roses in the garden. He went and plucked one. There was a clap of thunder and a furry beast appeared. "How dare you steal my rose!" he shouted.

"It's ... it's for my daughter Beauty," said the merchant. "She has a kind heart."

"A kind heart?" growled the Beast. "Then take this violet diamond and send her to me or you will die."

The merchant went home and told Beauty what had happened. She agreed to go to the castle. When she reached there, the rose flew back to the flower bed.

Beauty spent her days wandering around the castle. She found toys that spoke to her and lamps that glowed brightly. In one of the rooms she saw flutes, harps and violins that played on their own. Beauty loved this room the most and danced to the music every day.

One day, Beauty went to the library and began reading a book. Suddenly, she found the Beast standing before her. Seeing his sharp claws, she was afraid.

"Don't be afraid, Beauty," said the Beast gently. "I won't hurt you."

Soon they became good friends.

One night, Beauty had a dream that her father was ill. The Beast gave her a pearl ring and said, "Go see your father, but come back after twenty days. If you don't return, I will die. When you want to return, just twist this ring three times and you will be here."

Beauty thanked the Beast.

Beauty's father and her sisters were overjoyed to see her. She told them about the kind Beast.

Every day, Beauty fed her father hot soup and baked him cakes, pies and pastries. Soon he was well again. After a month had passed, Beauty remembered her promise.

Beauty said goodbye and rushed back. She saw the Beast lying lifeless. Teardrops from her eyes fell on the Beast and he woke up. Slowly his fur disappeared and he turned into a handsome young man. Her kindness had broken the spell. They got married and lived happily ever after.

The Emperor's New Clothes

Long, long ago there lived an emperor who was very fond of clothes. He liked to wear new clothes every day. He spent all day looking through his wardrobe for what to wear.

The emperor loved clothes so much that he had very little time for his people.

One day, when the emperor was sitting on his throne, a pageboy came in and said, "Two men want to see you."

The men told the emperor that they could weave the finest clothes in the world. "But our clothes have a magical quality. They cannot be seen by people who are fools," said one weaver.

The emperor was delighted to hear this. He said, "I would like you to make me some fine clothes for the grand procession next week."

He gave the weavers a large bag of gold and told his men, "Give these weavers silk threads of gold and silver and in all the colours of the rainbow."

Now these men were actually not weavers but wicked men who had come to cheat the emperor. They hid all the fine gold and silver threads that were given to them.

They dozed all day long, and pretended to weave only when someone came in.

A few days passed. The emperor wondered what his new robe looked like. He ordered his faithful old minister to go and see how the robe looked.

The minister walked slowly with the help of his walking stick till he reached the room where the weavers were working.

He entered the room and looked around. But he could not see anything. Then he rubbed his eyes, took out his spectacles, put them on and peered at the loom again. It was as empty as before.

Meanwhile, the two weavers pretended to be busy weaving. "Well, sir, do you like our work?" asked one weaver.

"Oh, it is beautiful!" replied the minister, who did not want the weavers to think he was a fool.

He went back and told the emperor that the robe was splendid. The emperor was happy and sent gifts to the weavers.

Now the emperor wanted to see the robe himself.

Next day, when the weavers saw the emperor come in, they pretended to cut some cloth and show it to the emperor. He blinked and rubbed his eyes.

'Oh dear! I cannot see anything. Am I a fool?' he thought. He pretended to take the cloth to the window to see it properly.

"This cloth is really marvellous," said the emperor at last. He went away, puzzled. But he had to keep quiet so that no one would think he was a fool.

The weavers went on pretending to cut with scissors and sew with needles. The candles in their room burned all night long.

On the day of the procession, the two weavers came to the emperor's room.

"Your Majesty, here is your new robe," said one weaver, as he pretended to hold it up proudly. "And my friend has your shirt, vest and trousers."

The emperor pretended to touch and admire the robe.

The emperor them took off his clothes. The weavers pretended to put on his new suit of clothes. The emperor stared at himself in the mirror. He could not see anything but dared not say so. All he could see were his underpants and crown. The emperor went out and took his place at the head of the procession.

Near the town hall, the emperor got down from his carriage. Everyone looked silently at the emperor.

Just then a child cried out, "Look, mother, the emperor is wearing nothing!" Then all the people started laughing. The emperor ran back to his palace in shame.

The Princess and the Pea

In a castle lived a king, a queen and their son, a very handsome young prince.

The prince wanted to marry, not just any princess, but a 'real' princess. He looked for her all over the world, travelling to many kingdoms but he could not find a real princess.

One day it began raining very heavily. Never in the last hundred years had it rained so hard in the kingdom. Thunder boomed and lightning flashed in the sky.

All the animals and birds were scared. They hurried as fast as they could to reach home or find shelter from the terrible storm.

The prince and his parents sat by the hearth wondering where they could find a real princess.

Suddenly they heard the clanging of bells. All of them were astonished. Who could it be?

The king took a lantern and went to tell the guard to open the door.

The guard saw a young girl standing at the door. Her clothes were torn and she was soaked and dripping. The guard took her to the king.

"Who are you, young lady?" asked the king.

"I am a princess. I have lost my way. May I stay here tonight?" asked the girl.

"Certainly," said the king, as he added a log to the fire.

The queen made her sit in a rocking chair near the fire and covered her with a rug. A bowl of steaming hot broth was given to her.

After having the hot broth, the girl said, "Thank you. That was good."

Meanwhile, the prince had fallen in love with the young girl the moment he set eyes on her. He wanted to marry her.

But the queen wanted to make sure that she was a real princess. She decided to test her. She ordered her maids to hide a tiny pea under twenty mattresses on the bed where the girl was to sleep.

When the clock chimed ten, the queen told the girl to go to bed. The maids took her to the bedchamber.

"Why is this bed so high?" she asked.

"To make you comfortable," the maids replied. The girl had to climb a ladder to get into bed. The maids went away, giggling.

At dawn, the queen woke up the king and the prince and they all got ready for breakfast.

"Where is the girl? The eggs and toast are getting cold," said the king.

"I'll go and call her," said the queen.

She climbed the ladder and found the girl sitting up wide awake.

"Come down, my dear," said the queen. "You look tired."

The girl said, "I don't want to be rude, but the bed was very uncomfortable. There was something hard under these mattresses. It poked me all night."

When the queen heard this, she smiled to herself.

The queen was glad that the girl was a real princess and she told the prince.

"Will you marry me?" asked the prince. The princess shyly agreed.

A herald was sent to the emperor and empress of Jura, informing them that the princess was safe. All the people were delighted.

So a grand wedding took place in the castle. The princess looked beautiful with a wreath of flowers in her hair and a bouquet in her hand. There was feasting all over the kingdom.

The king and the queen blessed the newly wed couple and so did the parents of the princess and their friends.

As for the pea, it became quite famous for it had helped to discover a 'real' princess. It was put inside a glass case and placed on a stand in the court for everybody to see. Villagers came from far and wide with their children to see the precious pea. And so the tiny pea became famous all over the world.